PuttinNwork Entertainment
Presents

ANTWON BRIDGES

BALAHMEAN

RISE
OF A
HUSTLER

This book is dedicated to my grandparents:
Mr. Jessie Bridges, Mrs. Lizzie Bridges, Mr. Lorenzo "Mack" Head,
my mother Karen Head Bridges,
my brother Neville Leon Bridges Jr. a.k.a. "Black",
my stepson Tyrone "Rex" Jeff...

Never judge the character of a Soulja, in a time of peace and prosperity.

Cause when there's no struggle and no threat everybody, profess to be loyal.

But in a time of struggle and a time of war you will witness true patriotism!!!

Acknowledgements

Being that this is my very first work of writing. As an author I want to thank God first and foremost. I want to thank our lord and savior for giving me life, for giving me a second chance to see all he has created on earth. Thank you lord, for giving me a second chance at life. Thank you lord for keeping your hands on me and not taking them off. Second, I would like to thank my beautiful, sexy, elegant, and classy, fiancée soon to be wife, Adriane Michelle Allen/Bridges. Babygirl you will always be my queen boo. Thanks for being there with your realness, trueness, love, and support. Yes the road got rough and hard at times but our love kept our relationship solid. Shell I will always be your ride or die man. I always tell you we are going to be alright. Now look at us baby-girl, we moving forward as one. I was always told to take it one day at a time, but as I started to see life myself, I learned I had to take it one moment at a time. I want to thank my Aunt Beck (Rebecca Cantrell) for always having my back no matter what. Thank you for the many weekends that you spent with me. We will always share a special bond together; yes you did everyday with me even through the struggle. I love you so, so much. A special thanks to my grandmother aka Momma to me. Thank you for being such a wonderful grandmother/mom. You never gave up on me, you al-ways believed in my dreams. Thank you for all the love and support that you give me. Other thanks to my big brother Neville Leon Bridges Jr. Aka black. I'm going to for-ever rep. You bruh it's always going to be. Long live black. If I did not put your name in this acknowledgement it ain't because I don't love you or fuck with you. It's just a long list of yall to name.

Special thanks to my fiancée and step son Tarrell Watson, I want to thank the both of y'all for the hours, days, weeks, and months, typing Balahmean Rise of a Hustler. All three of us put in a lot of work we still got two more books to drop before Balahmean's story is really told so let's do this and rep. Puttin NWoRk entertainment

Thanks to all my readers Balahmean is the bomb stay down two more is going to drop soon. Love always Joseph Antwon Bridges aka " Freedom".

TABLE OF CONTENTS

Chapter 1

"WHAT HAPPENED"

CHILLING DRIZZLING MISTED THE SCENE ALONG THE DRIVE WAY OF the three bedroom home as "Joseph Antwon Bridges", known throughout the neighborhood as "Balahmean" walked toward his father S.S. Impala that sat in the drive way mounted on 24 inch Chrome Rims. Balahmean was the eldest of his father two kids. His sister being 15 years old. Balahmean was 17 and at his age money was his only concern. His sister "Mia" came strolling out of the house holding her book bag slung over her left shoulder.

Bout time, Balahmean called back over his shoulder. "Whatever boy, don't rush me. You not my daddy" shouted back Mia. Opening the back door to her father S.S. Impala, "I never said that I was and don't wanna be either."

"Good, that makes two of us" she replied. "Y'all two don't start, it's too early in the morning. Now come on before you both be riding the bus, I got somewhere to be" said their father who name was "Valentino" as he watched them climb into his Impala.

"He started it" she wined sitting in the back of the car. "Stop lien" Balahmean said closing his father car door. "When y'all gone learn to get along with each" their father questioned pulling out their driveway. Balahmean and his sister both sat quiet not answering their father.

"Y'all gotta learn to love one another, cause at the end of the day y'all family. And you, you are her big brother and you act like you her age boy. You 17 years old and still play like you 12 years old it's time to grow up now boy. I ain't gonna be here to help guide your grown ass all your life, its time you take shit serious, or you'll fall victim to life" said Valentino schooling his son on life.

"You hear me son?"

"Yeah, I hear you Pops" said Balahmean really not listening to his father wisdom and knowledge.

"Your ass always talking about yeah, but this shit go in one ear and right out the other one" his father replied steering the Impala through the morning drizzle.

"Daddy, can I have five dollars for lunch" Mia asked.

"Yeah pumpkin" he answered pulling a bankroll of money from inside his vest coat pocket. "Here babygirl "he states given her a twenty dollar bill.

"Thanks' Daddy" Mia exclaimed happily to receive more than she needed.

"Yeah Pops, I need you to shoot me a dub too" said Balahmean mentioning his need for money.

"You ain't my girl and I damn sho ain't wake up with your ass in bed this morning" his father stated sincerely that cause Mia to burst out laughing loudly.

"Shut up" Balahmean "shouted" at his sister.

"Now your ass shut up! You need to find a job or something, cause you're a grown ass man almost and I ain't bout to be taken care of no grown ass man" his father shouted back sternly wanting him to realize everything wasn't a joke...

After getting fussed at by his father and laughed at by his baby sister. Balahmean jumped out his father Impala at the curb of "South Atlanta" High school drive way.

"Here" his father called out to him holding two twenty dollar bills. "Remember what I just told you, cause I ain't doing this no more. Bad enough I keep you fresh head to toe, but putting money in your pocket is all on you kid his father spoke driving off leaven him standing there dumb founded.

"Shit real" he mumbled tucking the money inside his blue jean Coogi pants.

Valentino was right; he couldn't always depend on his father for support. At some point he would have to grow up and do shit on his own. "What's up Balahmean? A familiar voice called out behind him. Balahmean turned to see his best friend "Twon" heading his way. What's up my nigga, Balahmean called back. Shit wassup look like pops done beat ya ears up dis morning. Hell yell, left me defenseless then a mu'fucka too bro. Balahmean, joked. I can tell said Twon as he and Balahmean made their way toward the school entrance.

So what's up with Sonya? Did you ever smash dat, he asked Balahmean curious. Naw, not yet. But I got them folks tho bro, we was on line almost four hours last night and she was digging all up in that pussy. "Word!" Twon spoke shocked, not believing his best friends word. That's on the hood homie;"Balahmean" lied through straight face. Sno'nuff I can't go for dat, not "Sonya" too goody good shoes from the expensive high life. "Twon "replied.

Yes, Sonya two goody good shoes from Austell, Georgia. Balahmean stated as if his words were true.

Sweet! Dat means you should be bussin her by the end of the week then, said Twon anxious for more detail. I guess so, I mean yeah. You guess so dude! You just had the baddest bitch at South Atlanta High School. She was finger fucking herself for almost an hour. How could you not get any play? You should be lucky for even maken it that far considering all the boys she downgraded and turned down, Twon mentioned.

Yea, you got a point, but women are sometimes unsure of themselves Balahmean replied trying to rectify his lie. He pulled off his book bag and sat it on the medal table next to Twon bag and watched it roll through the metal detector without a warnings sound of any weapons. They then were pat searched by the school officers before receiving their property. Are you going to eat breakfast or going to the gym? Asked Balahmean.

Um going to the gym dis morning, I ain't got no cash replied Twon. Say no more fool, you like my brother nigga. I got you bra, said Balahmean.

Ring, ring, ring! The bell loudly throughout the classroom announcing everyone to exit and heads toward the eating hall. Balahmean entered the lunchroom dressed in a coogi shirt and blue coogi jeans and all white Belair Jordan's on his feet. His hair was cut into a tempfade that made him look it like the great music Pioneer Doctor Dre.

About time this damn class period is over with umm ready to go Twon hissed dusting off his brand new 95 air max sneakers. Twon resembled the rapper Rich Homie Quan.

Um telling ya! Dese folks drownin a nigga with all this extra work for one little bitty ass math test, said Balahmean. As he stood in line, next to Twon waiting to purchased their lunch.

Ooh girl, look at his bum ass said Tanya joking and pointing at kids busted sneakers causing everyone to bust out in complete laughter. His shoes look like he been running track for three days. Balahmean chimed in with tears in his eyes. "Leave him alone" said Sonya appearing from nowhere not liken how everyone was picking at the boy shoes. Naw, that nigga been running for three years!" Hollered "Twon" still joking.

Where he got them shoes from? The thrift store another kid joked as they all made fun and joked around. Quit! Just stop it, damn enough already, Sonya screamed. Gathering everyone attention it's not funny, that could be one of you or y'all family. Everybody don't have as much as everyone should want them to never be quick to judge, cause the table could turn within a blink of an eye. Balahmean eye ballin knowing he was the center of it all despite their friendship, she hated boys who picked on the poor and it pained her to see it happen.

Aight aight ma, calm down babygirl said Tanya sarcastically. You should know out of all damn people that I dislike what y'all are doing said Sonya refocusing her attention on Balahmean okay baby damn he pleaded handing the lady behind the cashier. Giving his money for his food tray.

"No, um dead serious, you need to quit cause if the shoes was on the other foot, you'd be mad ya damn self. So what beat me at getting mad boy," she snapped walking off toward the eating table leaving him their lost in his own thoughts.

"Damn Bra! She just went dum ham on yo ass shawty" Twon laughed at him.

"Pleaseeee! You no ill go in on them folks. I just let her. Have the floor for a minute, ya dig? Sometimes you gotta let women blow their steam off or they'll end up hurting you in the end," Balahamean reached as if he knew it all

"I hear ya my nigga that shit sound real good. But I ain't who you need to be preaching too," He replied pointed in Sonya direction as she dumped her lunch into the garbage and headed out the lunchroom heatedly.

"Pssst, I don't give a fuck!" Balahmean lied. I ain't bout to be chasing no hoe about any bum ass nigga shoes. His people need to get a job or an extra one at lease." He stated playfully heading towards their everyday eating table...

The crowd grew enormous as kids hurried towards their awaiting school buses and parents. School was always overcrowded after being let out. Different groups of kids stood around waiting until their bus left campus.

"Bye Balahmean" said Tonya flirting as her school bus rode past him.

"Aight kool" he replied scanning his surroundings for his Dad's Impala. Which to no avail he didn't see amongst the other vehicles. "Damn! "

Where the fuck he at? He spoke to no one in particular. "I might gotta get on the bus then" he thought thinking of the last words his father had spoken that morning.

As Balahmean started for the Marta bus stop. He saw Sonya climbs into her mother blue Dodge Cara van a pull away. He stood next to the bus stop for nearly 15 minutes before the 78 Bus to "East Point" train station arrived. "Bout time" he thought getting on the bus swipe his school issued Marta card. He then took a seat next to an older woman who looked to be older than his great grandmother.

It took him a few minutes to get to the train station. He exited the Marta bus and made his way inside the station where he then waited on the train...

45 minutes passed and Balahmean was getting off the bus at the same exact time his sister after school program bus was letting her off at the end of the curb. "What up lil sis?" He spoke not wanting to argue with her, knowingly eventually they would end up bumping heads with one another, sooner or later. "Hey" she started to say but disturbed by a heavy sense of burning smoke. She coughed covering her mouth from the scent of the flames. "What da hell?" She managed to say through deep breathes as she saw the thick clouds rising into the air from a nearby home.

"Oh no! Somebody shit on fire" said Balahmean jokingly to his baby sister until they made it half way down the street near their house, then is where it hit him like a ton of blocks. Their house was indulged in thick blazing flames as black clouds of smoke rise in the air like tornadoes.

"Oh my God! Look!" Mia screamed backing away as the flames grew wilder sending strong wind of heat into their direction. People exited their homes as a fire truck and ambulance could be heard from a mile away.

"How da hell" Balahmean was cut off by the loud sound of a boom. Their house blew up into pieces as a neighbor grabbed them tight pulling them to safety. Fire trucks and polices cars swarmed and surrounded their house in luck at saving what little they could.

A throbbing headache grew as Balahmean sat on the next door neighbors porch lost in his own thoughts. Mia was inside "Mrs. Wilson's" home when the fire fighters, policemen, and crime scene investigators revealed the shocking news of discovering a male body amongst the burning ashes. Balahmean was startled at hearing the unsuspected bad news...

Chapter 2

"TABLES TURN"

Balahmean watched as they lowered his father's casket into the ground. Mia cried in disbelief as Mr. and Mrs. Wilson comforted her in everywhere possible. Crime scene investigators had found the male body to be their father and was said that a huge amount of gasoline was used to cause the fire. Balahmean sat frustrated not knowing or having a clue to as who could have wanted to kill and murda his father. He was partially disturbed the entire ceremony as his father last words etched through his mind. Mrs. Wilson caressed his back and shoulder in effort to help him remain strong.

Him not having a lot of relatives caused for a very small funeral. He looked over at his baby sister and immediately recognized her current state of loss and depression. He vowed to take care of her from there on out with his every will to live as his father wanted them to, or die poor. He took one last glance at his father black and brown wood grain sliver casket that Mr.

and Mrs. Wilson purchased with no expense and mumbled "Real niggas don't die, they sleep"...

Later that evening they were situated at Mr. and Mrs. Wilson's two bedroom home as she prepared dinner for celebrity purposes. Her saying was "why worry when losing a close relative where you should be celebrating their happiness?" Mr. and Mrs. Wilson had given them a roof over their heads and a place to stay. They'd known his father for almost 11 years and had come to love them as well as they did his father.

Mia thoughts were interrupted as she drifted down memory lane. "You okay sis?" He asked more outta concern than conclusion despite their past arguments they were family and it was time for them to love each other as one.

"Not really," she responded sadly submitting her feelings of grief and emotion.

"Alright, um here if you need me," he kissed the top of her forehead and hugged her tightly as he rocked her back and forth in his arms.

She started to cry freely as her brother held her close for dear life. They'd both experienced a tragedy like this before from losing their mother. He caressed the natural curls of his sister delicate hair. One glance was all it took to reestablish the connection between them. Their bond was unbreakable.

He released her from his grasp just as Mr. Wilson came walking into what used to be their guests room.

"You kids alright in here?" He asked with a deep husky voice from his currently condition. Mr. Wilson was diagnosed with cancer and sickle cell.

"Yes, we're fine. Just a lot of pressure is all," Mia managed to say with grievance emotion.

"Alright, dinners ready. You two come on down and put something on your stomachs." He replied leaving the room as he ascended the stairs.

Mia unleashed a long full of air as she flapped down on the queen size bed. "It's not fair" she pleaded. "I know but we have to continue to live, now let's go eat." He stated reassuringly... Balahmean was awakening the next morning almost at 6:30 by Mrs. Wilson today was their first day of school since their father death. And Balahmean was more than just nervous. He was unstable. He pulled back the thick bed covers and climbs from outta the queen size bed, making his way towards the hallway bathroom by passing his sister who was always ready and on time for school. Mrs. Wilson had calmly awakened her as well. "Good morning," he replied disappearing inside the bathroom. "Hi Mrs. Wilson. Good morning," said Mia dressed in one of the many outfits she'd been given by Mrs. Wilson. She and her brother was forced to wear hand me downs not having anything to their name as the fire burned everything to ashes, including their father and his belongings. "Good morning their beautiful," she greeted back admiring the dress she'd given to Mia.

"Just tryna take everything one day at a time, is all," Mia spoke genuine taking a seat at the dining room table.

Balahmean finished brushing his teeth and entered their guestroom where he had his clothes already hang on the back arm of the chair. Mr. Wilson had given him a flick color shirt and clad shorts to wear to school and him being the top notch nigga he was he declined the offer, instead he told her he would only rewash his remaining stunning outfit that he wore the day of their house fire. It had been almost two weeks since he'd last been to school and his hair was now in deep rows of naps and his Bel-Air Jordan sneakers were slightly dirty from both having the effort to clean or keep them washed. He redressed in his coogi outfit and made his way down the steps where Mia and Mrs. Wilson were sitting at the table chattering away as they ate breakfast.

"You hungry, baby?"

"Yes ma'am," he responded rubbing his stomach through the front of his shirt indicating that he was indeed ready to eat.

He sat beside his sister while Mrs. Wilson fixed his plate of grits, eggs, bacon, toasted bread, and homemade buttermilk biscuits with some grape jelly.

Mr. Wilson was off to work at his local retail shop on Main Street in College Park, Ga.

You okay, lil sis?" "Yeah, um slowly pulling through. How bout you? You doing okay, sure look like you could use another day of restless sleep," she joked playfully tryna make light of their current situation. (Laughs) "You right bout that, um tired as hell."

"Watch your profanity young man," Mrs. Wilson chimed in.

'Yes ma'am, I apologize Mrs. Wilson" he replied vulnerable turning his attention back to his sister.

"So, see you ready for school" Mia asked skeptically.

"Don't know, why" he questioned.

"No reason at all, just asking. I'm kind of afraid myself, but I'll do just fine I guess," she replied as Mrs. Wilson sat the plate of food down in front of Balahmean.

"Thank you Mrs. Wilson, for everything" he stated before saying his grace.

By 7:45 a.m. Mrs. Wilson was dropping them off at school at the same exact time three other school buses were releasing a crowd of teenagers on school campus.

Mrs. Wilson bright candy apple red 1971 Cadillac seemed to be the center of attention as different crowds of people pointed and laughed at her car.

Balahmean was embarrassed from all the attention her car caused.

I should have ridden the Marta bus. He thought as she pulled alongside of the curb. Mia sadly looked out her back seat window as the long bed Cadillac came to a screeching stop.

"You kids have fun and enjoy yourselves, okay" said Mrs. Wilson seeing the change in their mood swing.

"Aight" Balahmean stated sternly exiting the car with attitude. "Bye Mrs. Wilson" Mia called back ready to get as far away as she could from the bright red car Mrs. Wilson now drove.

'Be good now, y'all hear" she yelled out to them before finally driving away in route to her job at the C.V.S. pharmacy located on Washington Rd. in East Point, GA.

"What kind of car that was? A spaceship!" A kid hollered causing the entire crowd to bust out in laughter.

"Naw that was a space rocket!" said another kid cracking a joke of his own. Balahmean ignored their comments as he and Mia made their way through the entrance of the school.

"Ain't that the same outfit, he wore last week" some kid called out.

"Yep, and look at his busted ass Jordans. He needs a damn haircut," another kid yelled loudly.

Balahmean turned to see who the kid was and came face to face with the kid he been joken on the week before. The kid had his earlobes pierced, his haircut and brand new clothes and shoes to go along. Balahmean just stood there quiet and dumb founded not having anything to say. He felt lonely and concerned as everyone lashed out different jokes about him now being poor due to the fact that his house burned down. He regretted ever making fun of the kid as thoughts of Sonya evaded his mind. And as he was lost in deep thoughts Sonya came passing by. She gave him a look of disgust and at the moment he vowed that he'd rather "Get rich" than "Die broke".

"Yo, what's up fool?" Said Twon outta nowhere.

"Shit, bout to skip school bro. Uma fuck with you tomorrow shawty, I gotta go see somebody" Balahmean replied dapping his friend with a handshake.

"Aight fam let me know if you need me my nigga. What's mines is yours fool" said Twon noticing Balahmean appearance was off beat. "I know bra, um gucci shawty. You the fucking worst "said Balahmean heading back out the school doors in route to a mysterious destination.

Mia watched quietly as her brother left the school building...

Chapter 3

"JUMPING SHIFT"

"BALAHMEAN" HAD SKIPPED SCHOOL THE PREVIOUS DAY AND arrived at Popeye's house in College Park, Ga. Popeye was one of his other close friends from Crossroad Alternative School for bad behavior kids who indulged in skipping class and school fighting. Popeye was also 17 years old standing 5'9 paperback brown complexion favoring the rapper of Texas Mike Jones. He was known for pushing big weight throughout the neighborhood of College Park and East Point Georgia.

Popeye had given Balahmean a blacksmith 38 special that fit into the palm of his hand with ease. Balahmean eyed the piece of steel as he stood on the side of Charles corner store on Harvard Avenue in College Park Georgia. He'd cut a black skullcap into a skimask and had it stuck into his back pants pocket. It was only 9:30 in the morning and Charles was late arriving at his corner store at a quarter past nine. He parked his brown tan Lexus CLS in front of the store and climbed out making his way up the parking lot. In his left hand he held a Louis Vuitton tote bag. He would usually make his first round trip at the First International Bank on Main Street. Charles was a middle age black man, short and stocky favoring "worm" on Friday the movie. He walked up approaching his store digging into his coat pocket for the keys. Within a matter of seconds he was sticking the key into the door lock with his right hand as he held the Louis Vuitton bag on the other side. Balahmean jaw tensed and his facial expressions changed from in securities to self-survival. His adrenaline was now at an all-time high as a cold chill ran down his spine. Click was the sound of the door being unlocked as Charles slowly opened the door with caution. Balahmean arriving outta know where coughed violently announcing his presence. Charles turned at the sound and came face to face with a smith western 38 special "you know what it is ole man, don't be a hero. Just come off the loop, Balahmean demanded as Bain's could be seen all over his forehead. Don't kill me! Get whatever you want. Charles yelled as people could be seen across the street in an empty parking lot, "shut the fuck up!", Balahmean spoke calmly bringing the butt of the revolver down over the man's nose, causing thick layers of blood to ooze down his mouth. There was a gash over the brim of his nose as he hollered. Come on with that check said Balahmean once more grabbing him by the collar of his button down dress shirt. He pressed the barrel of the gun into his mid-section before asking again. Pussy, nigga run that check! Charles jerked away roughly hollering all kinds of profanity gestures causing a small scene. Boom! The blast from the revolver echoed throughout the morning peace. Balahmean felt Charles go limp as he cried out in pain. The bullet ripped through his intestinal blowing a hole in his lung as he kept a grip on the bag for almost dear life. Boom the second bullet bashed into Charles skull splattering his brains all over the door frame of the store. Car horns beeped loudly as they struggled to get a better view of the scene.

Balahmean stood shocked for a few seconds from the unhealthy fixation. It was his first kill and the only robbery while his stomach began to boil. Shit he huffed as brain juice rolled toward his shoe causing a trail of yellow fluid. He reached down and snatched the Louis Vuitton bag from Charles dead and lifeless hand and took off running full speed around the side of the corner store. Balahmean had parked a stolen blue Honda Accord at the back side of the store. A loud screech could be heard as he rounded the corner causing him to look back and catch sight of a blue college park police cruiser coming to a halt at the front of the store. He almost panicked in disbelief from regretted but still he managed to keep moving, jumping a fence and crossing over a neighbor yard. He rushed to the driver seat of the Honda. A second police car could be seen at the end of the street heading in the opposite direction. Quickly, he climbed into the car forcing the flathead screwdriver inside the broken ignition as his hand trembled. Mustering the patience to be still. He twisted the screwdriver towards the right and brought the car to life. He floored the gas pulling away from the curb making his getaway. He shook involuntary from nervousness. The interior of the car was wet from his sweat, as he rode in silence. He replayed the whole scenario over and over again in his head. He couldn't shake feeling of knowing he'd killed his first human being that made his entire body pulse with paranoia. He came upon another stoplight and saw an ambulance fly passing him in massive speed. His lips quivered not knowing how to adjust to what had just taken place. He had spazzed physically his mind felt manipulated than psycho>His heart rapidly as he hung a left on to old national in outta in route to motel 6. Slouching in his seat he still held the bag in his hand the entire way. The gun was tucked I his pants pocket. He wanted to unzip the bag and peep in to it out of curiosity, but thought against it feeling a sinful bliss. He fantasized about being rich with lots of beautiful, fine women's and fancy cars. But was soon interrupted by an awaiting vehicle behind him at the red-light. Beeeeepp!!!! Balahmean purchased an overnight at the motel 6 for forty dollars and sixty-eight cent total. He left the Honda parked outside backward incase a squad car drove past and just so happened to run the license plates. He sat on the sofa plush motel bed as old cigarette smoke could be smelled from all the years of installation. A small television was mounted on top of a worn down dresser near the one and only bathroom. A cheap rocking chair was pushed into the corner of the right side of the room.

Balahmean totaled the money to be exactly twenty-two thousand. He nodded to himself in the nearby full length floor mirror and flashed the brightest smile that had ever decorated his face since the death of his father. A to his promise he loved the new feeling it's like his whole life had suddenly changed within a blink of an eye. The world seemed to not exist as he got lost in his thoughts. Brightness overwhelmed him for a minute, until the cold hearted death of his father resurfaced with everlasting darkness.

He admired the stacks of money neatly layer out on the bed and instantly felt they deserved more. Despite him having enough to get through the rainy days. He knew a time like this would come again. Slowly he unscrewed and twisted the top off a Pepsi drink bottle and gulped long and deeply. His mouth was dry and he was indeed dying of thirst. He shuffled the money into one large pile and sat it on the side nightstand. After standing up and making his way to the sink, he twisted the noob cutting on the cold water letting it run for a split second before splashing cold water on to his face. He shook his head from side to side and stated "Uma get rich, or die broke" as he stared at his self in the mirror. He fidgeted from recognizing the killer within himself he never knew was there. Life wasn't too bad for him, after all except for the death of his father. His dickie long sleeve shirt was tossed over the arm of the chair seated in the corner of the motel room. Blood was smeared across it from the blast he sent through Charles head. His pants were neatly folded in the chair and he wore only gym shorts made by Michael Jordan and his Nike socks. Picking up the remote control to the rugged television, he flipped through a series of channels stopping at espn sport center. Time seemed to be changing for the better, after all only one thing was on his mind get rich. There were certain things he'd do in order to become rich and sitting still wasn't one of them. He stayed cooped up inside the motel the entire day as he thought of ways to get money. He not only wanted to become rich, but he wanted his earnings to still be maximizing even after he'd die. So that his lil sister would be legit for life...

Early the next morning, he was wide awake and ready for action as he checked out the motel and climbed into the Honda. He stuck the key inside the ignition and heard the engine come to a silent roar. Pulling out into the morning traffic, he headed straight for Capone used car lot which Jay owned off metropolis. Almost 20 minutes passed by before Balahmean swung the stolen vehicle into Jay's car lot. A white middle aged couple came strolling out with the look of happiness on their faces. There was a series of new model cars lined along the front parking lot. Benzes, BMW, Lexus, Porches and Range Rovers some were mounted high on silver, gold and platinum rims. He parked the Honda beside a 2 door t-top1978 chey chevell that sat mounted up on 24 inch ashunt rims.

That bitch there stupid is stupid, said Balahmean while getting outta the car seeing Jay talking to a customer about business. What's up big homie? He called out causing Jay to turn at the sound of his voice. Jay looked not recognizing who was talking to him off back. Nigga, what the hell you doing out this way? I ain't seen yo lil ass since last Christmas, Jay barked. I know shawty but minus the bullshit life's great. Um tryna cop a whip big homie, he confused cutting the small talk. Just like your dad nigga, always ready to handle business. I like that young nigga. Oh! By the way my condolence goes out to pop's. I heard the news, whoever did that shit gonna get it. You can believe that, Jay replied with anger in his voice. True that, same here homie. But what you tryna let that go for. He stated pointing his index finger in the direction of the T-Top Chevy chevell the candy apple red paint job looked as if it was dripping wet. Oh that bitch on the market for 15 bands but I tell you what lil nigga. I'll give it to you for 12 thousand. Do to the fact me and your Pop's were best men, Jay stated seriously. "Sho'nuff! Stop playing big homie, said Balahmean not believe him. I ain't bullshitin lil nigga. Take it or leave it said Jay. One look is all it took for him to know Jay was fo real. Run it, Balahmean replied already reaching inside his pocket fo the cash amount. He pled off the 12 thousand

and handed it to him quickly. Where you get this kinda money from lil nigga, what you selling crack now? Jay asks confusingly. Come on now homie, you no better than that, said Balahmean with an assuring smile that could pass for the devil himself. Oh yeah I can dig it lil homie, but if you change yo mind one day. You know I got it straight drop, Jay boasted heading behind the desk of a computer top. Look fills these papers out and you good to go lil nigga.

Alright say no more, replied Balahmean filling out the paperwork and title to his new whip. Oh yeah, you beta come back and get this hit ass car out of my parking lot too. Jay demanded through straight face. Alright done deal, said Balahmean as Jay handed him his car keys...

Chapter 4

"JUST BEGUN"

AFTER PURCHASING HIS FIRST CAR, JAY LEFT HIM WITH TEN THOU-sand totals. He drove the car with windows down as lyrics from the up and coming rapper "Young Thug" blasted throughout his stereo system. He caught glances from a group of girls all jammed packed inside a green ford tarus. He threw up his hand to indicate a formal greeting of what's up. The stop light changed from red to green and he smashed through burning rubber as he saw the group of girls tryna to keep up but couldn't manage. Smiles to himself he knew he'd chosen the right path. Within 10 minutes he was pulling alongside Mrs. Wilson Cadillac. It was now 8:56 in the morning and he'd suspected for Mia to be already at school. But to his surprise there she stood. Hand on her left hip as if she was about to blow steam from her ears. Where the hell you been at? Everybody been looking for you boy, Charles was murdered yesterday and someone claim to have saw you at his store. At the same exact time he was killed. Mia stated delivering the news of the chaos. Don't believe shit you hear girl. Why aren't you in school, that's what I want to know? He questioned her. She answered by saying that I was waiting on you. I didn't know where you were, "so I thought it could be true". She replied speaking the truth.

Well you were wrong, now get dressed we are going to the mall, with what money. She snapped recognizing his car for the very first time. Who car Mia asked looking puzzled. Balahmean stated mines I just bought it. You remember daddy's friend Jay don't you? Well he let me scoop it for a little of nothing on behalf of daddy. He submitted as a bright smile spreader across his face. Wow said Mia you done turned it up to the next level. Hell yeah most definitely we gotta grind our way from the bottom and back where we belong. He preached following her inside the house. Mr. and Mrs. Wilson were both at work giving them time and space they'd been wishing for.

Balahmean sat outside the women's dressing room and admired almost every outfit his baby sister tried on. She went from coach to Louis Vuitton, Gucci, apple bottom and Prada. He enjoyed the smile of seeing Mia face light up. He didn't see that kind of happiness on her face since there father was living. Thoughts of his father invaded his mind as he watched Mia emerge from the women room dressed in a Derlon mini short skirt that made her favor "Teyana Taylor".

How do I look? She questioned obviously not paying attention to his mood swing. Beautiful, he lied not that she didn't but because he wasn't paying her the slightest attention. Balahmean mind had begun to wonder off into space sometimes and he wondered was he actually losing his sense of humor. A dark skin thick lady came from behind the women's room ass poking out her jeans as if they were bout to bust open. He silently stood to his feet sitting down his shopping bags. He headed in her direction determined to introduce himself. As he was about to approach her man called after her from his right and he instantly fell back...

After leaving the Saks Fifth Mall at Lenox, Balahmean and Mia met up with Melissa to put down on an apartment in Buckhead called Avalon

Ridge. They bought a modest but yet expensive piece of property that came fully stocked from black leather wrapped around living room sofas and two master bedroom with plush king sized beds. A dining set that matched the marble brown hardwood floors and three separate 42inch plasma screen in every room. Two bathrooms and an outdoor swimming pool unable to take her eyes off of the beautiful apartment. Mia enjoyed the wonderful Victorian home for the first time. The Wilson's were both hurt by them leaving so unexpected, but they were indeed happy for them and to see a smile flash across their face made them even happier. Balahmean parked his tinted window chevell beside the curb next to a school bus as teenagers wondered who could be driving the car. Everyone started exiting their buses in route toward school. As Balahmean began to play music from the car turning up the volume as loud as it would go. Causing the ground and car to vibrate words from the rapper "Trinidad James" could be heard clearly. Don't believe me just watch! Don't believe me just watch! Gold all in my chain! Gold all in my rang! Gold all in my watch! Don't believe me just watch! Mia climbed out first with her hair pulled back into a bun, dressed in a jimmy choo outfit and heels. Balahmean jumped out wearing a true religious jean outfit with a pair of baleneiago sneakers on his feet. A crowd of whispers and unwanted stares shot their way. Balahmean caught sight of Sonya walking hand in hand with the same kid who was making fun at him just the other day. As it turned out what goes around come back around because he'd been joking at the kid first. He flashed a none hard feeling smile as he leaned inside the car and killed the noise by withdrawing the key from the ignition. This you said Tonya admiring his new car. She ran her hand along the hood of his car seductively before speaking to Mia who was now heading toward the school building. Yeah this me, he responded grabbing his writing tablet from the seat. I love it, its beautiful make me wet. She ran her tongue across her top lip starring him intensely in the eyes for what seemed forever. Mia disappeared inside the school amongst the crowd of teenagers.

Sho nuff I hear that. Balahmean stated amused at her flamboyant um hungry wanna grab something to eat from McDonald's. She said not really wanting to get something to eat. Shit it don't matter, let's dip he replied turning toward his car. She climbed in beside him as he cranks the engine, music blasted almost busting her eardrums as he lowered the volume steering the vehicle out into the morning traffic. She stuck her hand over and rested it between his thighs. Got some where we can go? She whispered sexily biting her bottom lip. Balahmean dick spranged to life feeling her unzipping his pants. We can go to my spot, he stated as she pulled him free and went down...

* * *

Balahmean and Tonya returned to school a little later than 9:35 she had given him pleasure the entire drive home. The results ended with him blasting his everlasting seed inside her love box. They'd went at it none stop for almost an hour straight without any breaks or rest. Balahmean was now inside the school bathroom shooting dice. Shoot fifty bet fifty more said Twon who was shooting the dice against Black, the kid who'd they made fun of a couple weeks ago.

Black was dark skin, he resembled "meek mills." Aight say no more, Black replied taking the bet. He shook the dices inside his hand before releasing them up against the bathroom wall. One dice landed on a five and the other one continued to spin before landing on a two. Damn yelled Black cramping out loosen his money and side bets. That's what um talking bout, said Balahmean spit picking up his winnings. Loving the pitiful look on Black face. Bet back Black asked wanting a chance to win his money back from Balahmean. He had won two hundred and eighty-three dollars from Black. Black felt that he deserved another shot at his money. Um straight my nigga, it's over with said Balahmean thumbing through a fist full of bills. Damn! It's like that shawty? Black right hand man Blue started eye balling Balahmean as he counted his money. Even though he only had a total of nine hundred and a few loose bills. He always kept his money in his back pocket. The two hundred and eighty three dollars was in his front pocket, as he finished adding up his total. It's over with I ain't shooting no more! Balahmean spit not carrying about Blue reputation as a bully and bad ass.

You gonna give my man another shot at his money, Blue huffed out of anger. Hold up playa, who the fuck you talkin to like that nigga! Twon spit defensive other niggas just stared on in amusement at Twon bold comment.

Nigga you know y'all don't want no smoke, just come up off that check before one of y'all fool's get beat to sleep. Blue responded aggressively. Balahmean stood there only smiling at first until Blue slid behind him silently and tossed him into a massive choke hold with his forearm. Nigga you! Twon was cut off at the sound of Black other partner. Yank unfolding a switch blade. Bus a move punk, Yank demanded as Blue choked Balahmean unconscious and went into his front pocket and pulled out all his winnings. I appreciate that lil nigga; he stated laying down Balahmean on the nasty bathroom floor. Twon was heated as they all left the bathroom leaving only him and Balahmean to themselves. He shook him repeatedly tryna awake him from his unconscious seeing that it didn't help. He turned on the cold water and dashed Balahmean across his face. Splash! What the fuck! Balahmean yelled as the cold water awoke him. He bottled up right. He was still dreaming drunk. His heart pounded from the horrible memory of what just happened. Now as he slowly gaining some form of groggy consciousness. He gained his focus and stood to his feet. You good bro? Twon asked through gritted teeth helping his partner up from the floor. Uma kill that nigga, is all he replied as he rolled paper towels off the wall to dry his wet face. Twon was at an all-time list of words cause he too was angered at how they'd handle the situation. Now things could go haywire at any given moment. He already had learned beforehand what Balahmean was capable of doing from the Charles event. Consider it done said Twon meaning every word. He followed Balahmean out the school as kids roamed the halls and teachers scurried on about their day. They made it outside the school and got inside his car and peeled away.

After they left school, Balahmean took Twon to his granddaddy house on Victoria Street in College Park to get his strap. He waited as his friend took time at getting his belongings. Fifteen minutes passed and Twon came out holding his waistline. Got it he told Balahmean broadcasting the silver 380 Larkin hand pistol. I like that mu'fucka bra that bitch stupid hard Shawty. Twon closed the car door as they drove away. Balahmean pulled up to the B.P gas station on Cleveland Avenue and loaded his tank with sixty dollars' worth of gas. He then purchased a small five dollars box of cigarillos and a pack of Newport cigarettes. Twon grabbed a coke and a pack of skittles. After pumping the gas tank they pulled off toward south town apartments. It didn't take long before Balahmean swerved the chevell into the rough neighborhood. He stopped the car and climbed out. I'll be back, he told Twon ushering himself to the apartment building. After knocking on the door twice. Tony answered the door dressed in all white Armani linen with white Armani gators on his feet. Tony was a pecan tan skin guy with natural curly hair. What's up playboy said Balahmean. Spit giving him some dap. Shit high to death what you tryna get lil bra? Tony asked opening the door for him to enter the house. Give me a seven of that pineapple kush and a seven of the mango kush. I don't want that air pack either. He joked sharing a small laugh.

Lil nigga pleaseee! I don't sale any air pack. You gotta go holla at Randy bout that. Tony spit playfully speaking of unk from Victoria Street in the white duplex house on the hill. He walked off and headed into the kitchen and returned with two zip lock bags of loud, known as marijuana to America. Smell like that gas too said Balahmean sniffing the bag for that smell. He loved deeply more than ever. That's all I prefer Tony spit... Balahmean reached into his back pocket and peeled off two hundred and thirty dollars and handed it to him. What's this is? Tony said examine the shortage of his cash next time lil nigga come with the whole two fifty. Tony split watching Balahmean sternly. Aight, I got you playboy. You know us well for it shawty, oh and tell Ms. Dacia I said to get at me. Balahmean spit of his sister then left... He inhaled a cloud of smoke as he and Twon waited on school to be let out.

Ringggg! The school bell sounded loudly as kids hurried and raced for their assigned buses. Small group of kids stood round holding conversations with their girlfriend, boyfriend, friends and family members. They saw Blue and Yank emerge from the school side exit door. Balahmean had already told his sister to ride the bus home cause of his mishap. There they nigga's go right there, said Twon pointed out through the large crowd of teenagers. I see them he nodded. They watched Blue climb into the passenger side of Yank old school smoke grey cutlass with the burgundy rag top. The reverse eight's and vol's sitting bowlegged as Yank pulled off out of the school parking lot. Balahmean drove behind them in an unmarked Nissan Maxima. They bought from a kid name E-man. He maneuvered the car two rows back, sure to be kept outta sight. Yank came to a red-light and was in a deep conversation when Balahmean and Twon jumped out in the middle of oncoming traffic and rushed alongside the car. Balahmean ranned to the passenger side and tapped on the window. Blue swung his head around and thought he'd seen a living ghost. Before he had a chance to plead Balahmean stated was "ya life worth it nigga."

Twon had surprised Yank by busting open his driver window with the butt of his gun. Pow! Pow! Bullets from Twon 380 slammed into yank chest knocking air from his lungs. Cars stopped taking in the horrible scene as many dialed 911 for assistance. Please my nigga, I got a baby on the way shawty Blue begged from the heart as Balahmean snatched open the car door. He roughly grabbed him by the collar of his shirt and tossed him out the car onto the pavement.

Boom! He sent a slug through Blue hand as he tried to hold it up forming an unusual shield. Agh! Blue screamed out in pain hoping someone would help him make it through his nightmare. Boom! Blood splashed all over the concrete as a hole was now formed at the nape of Blue neck. He squeezed and squirmed come on bra. Let's go! Twon hollered out in fear as he heard police siren's nearby. Balahmean seemed to be in his own world as he stared. Blue intensely in his dark brown eyes. Nigga you robbed me, now um bout to return the favor fucks man. Balahmean spit harshly aiming his gun at the center of Blue forehead. He tried to mumbled something but was cut short by the lighting bullet "Balahmean " sent between his eyebrow an eyeball somehow managed to pop from its pocket and Balahmean crushed it with the bottom of his shoe. Let's go! Twon hollered again. This time tuggin him by his shirt sleeve. Balahmean barely heard a word he said as he fired another shot into Yank body for good measure as they rushed to the car. Twon jumped behind the wheel and stomped on the gas pedal watching the meter go from zero to sixty-five miles an hour.

Are you crazy? He barked at his friend paranoid" mite is", Balahmean smiled back viscously with a cold hearted grin. Twon jumped on the expressway and gunned the engine...

Chapter 5

"CODE OF SILENCE"

BALAHMEAN AND TWON BOTH RETURNED TO SCHOOL THE FOLLOW-
ing day as if nothing had taken place. Twon was slightly paranoid from
time to time from his first experience at murder. Balahmean however on
the other hand could care less about what they'd do yesterday. They caught
all kinds of glances and stares from other girls and teachers. It had been
rumored that Blue had robbed Balahmean the previous day, so more than
likely he caught most of the attention .Twon was in the clear. Balahmean
was sitting at the computer board in social studies class when out of
nowhere the school assigned police officer Blake known as Mack throughout the neighborhood came strolling into the classroom with another uniformed cop close by. Mr. Cory Taylor can you please stand and come with
us. The white uniformed cop stated for what, "Balahmean" questioned
nervous feeling his adrenaline start to kick. You're wanted for questioning
said Mack as silence filled the air. Everyone in the class just looked; Jarvis

dropped mouth open as if they'd never seen this type of shit before. He looked around and caught Sonya glaring at him in hatred. He smiled as he calmly stood up and stated" make it quick, I got shit I gotta do." Watch your tongue, Cory said Mrs. Porter his home room teacher. Mack walked beside him as the other cop led the way down the hall and out the school. Mia was at lunch when a girl called out. They got "Balahmean" they got your brother! Mia looked and saw the school officer and another cop both walking her brother out the school. She dropped her tray on the table as all eyes were fixed on her next movement. She took off at full speed toward the front entrance catching them as they were opening the back door for him to climb inside. Wait she hollered causing the white cop to look back immediately. Who are you? He questioned her. He's my brother, stupid! What it look like, she responded smartly with an attitude and worries all at once. What's going on? She demanded seeing her brother standing there with a smirk on his face. He's wanted for questioning ma'am was to escort him to our local prescient, said Mack. Questioning for what? For the murder of Scott Reese and Steve Gram, he replied. Everything Gucci lil sis, I ain't did shit. Go ahead and finish school.

I'll be back when they done with their useless questioning. Balahmean assured with a devilish smirk on his mouth. Okay, but if they decided to do anything, call me A.S.A.P aight. She spoke not wanting him to go along, but didn't have any choice regardless of what she wanted. Aight, love you lil sis, he professed reassuringly with a wink of his right eye. Love you too bra, tell them what they want and hurry back, she said replied knowing he knew what she meant as don't tell them a damn thing. He winked his eye as he got into the back seat and said, "Get rich or die broke" she knew none of what he meant....

Down at the prescient Balahmean was brought to a concrete room with a steel table and a steel chair. There was a sound proof glass board where they heard everything you said. You just couldn't hear them. He sat in the steel chair slouched eyes glued to the pizza they'd offered him minutes ago. They know he was a prime suspect and that alone gave them reasons to try and intimidate him. But Balahmean wasn't a rookie to the crime life. He'd had his share of court dates and detention center. He knew the code of o'merta as the Italians put it. Keeping quiet was the rule of crime bosses and tells meant you were a coward and couldn't stand the pressure. Where were you at 3:38 yesterday afternoon? Detective Jones asked awaiting his answer. Balahmean stood there blank starring at the now cold pizza. He declined. I just told you the same shit thirty minutes ago, listen Mr. or should I just say detective Jones. You can quite with all the back and forth shit my nigga, cause um not changing anything I've already done told you. So to save your ass by ending this here session. Balahmean spoke uncut without any sugar coating. You're a smart ass huh? They gonna sentence you to life without parole and I hope them boy's fuck your inside so good you'll need crutches for the rest of your miserable life Jones stated. You know what detective Jones that was pretty impressive and I honestly think you should win pump faking officer of the year award, on show time at the Apollo. Balahmean spit with laughter as he cracked himself to death. He was laughing so hard that his eye's began to water as if he was about to cry. Shut your fucking mouth, before I charge you with, withholding evidence said Jones frustrated letting his emotions get the best of him. His face had turned stone cold red as sweat began to poor down his forehead. He discreetly headed out the room still hearing Balahmean remarkable laugh that pissed him off even more. That's one smart mouth ass kid. I wish him the best of luck cause one day somebody gonna put him where he needs to be, and that's the graveyard. Detective Jones stated harshly to Officer Blake and his partner walking pass them heatedly.

Balahmean sat at the table thinking of how he'd just reversed the game on detective Jones. It was for them to get him mad and upset. But by him being young tolerant, he manipulated Jones into angering himself far enough to lose focus of his main objective. I should have gone to law school. He mumbled at the presentation he'd just performed on detective Jones. A tall brown complexion detective came bargin through the door dressed in trousers held up by suspenders and a white APD write beater that was nudged by a twin set gun harness. He appeared to be federal and much abused. Sign here kid, and you're free to go, he stated. What am I signing sir. I want an attorney present before I put my lingo on anything I don't understand. He reasoned before being let go...

Balahmean had declined their offer of returning him to school. Instead he rode the bus. He arrived on campus at 1:40 in the afternoon. Class periods were now in rotation as he walked along the busy hallways acknowledging all kinds of unwanted attention. He couldn't help but love the fame. He was now receiving from the entire school, including the teachers. You good bra? Booker asked. A nigga from around the Newman, Ga area. Yea um Gucci fam, Preciate the concern replied Balahmean swaggerly. No doubt, he stated heading towards the gym. He spotted Twon coming from the west end of the school with his girlfriend Tiffany from eagles homes projects in zone one Atlanta. They were both entwined in a conversation. Welcome back brother she playfully joked hugging him tight. Preciate it sis said Balahmean truthfully. Those crackers tried to railroad a playa. He joked. Sho'nuff so everything Gucci? Twon asked referring to them being in the clear. Yeah man we Gucci my nigga. Say Tiffany I though you said you had an older sister that you were gonna hook me up with. See you be flexing too much said Balahmean.

I do! I do! I tell you what come over to my house with us after school, and I'll let you do the rest. Deal said Balahmean. She suggested. Fucking right don't be playa hating when you see big sister tryna give me the pussy either, he joked as they all busted out laughing. Boy! Whatever my sister is grown. I can't tell her who do not have an affair with replied Tiffany. My man right here now gives me a kiss she told Twon as their mouth met. Y'all need to get a room or some. Y'all little freaky ass? Balahmean spit laughing we grown and we don't need a room. We need a country she laughed playfully as they continued on down the hall in route to their classes.

Balahmean was anxious to meet Tiffany older sister and couldn't wait. He almost grew impatient as he told himself today would officially be his last day of school. College never existed to him anyway. All he ever wanted to do was be like his father. He'd become addicted to ballin and shining for no way possible was School gonna stop him from eating. His birthday was next week and he would be eighteen. Class periods flew by faster than any other day and Balahmean was disturbed by the ringing of the school bell. Announcing that school was officially over for today. He gathered his writing pad and moved passed moving teenagers as he walked up to Mrs. Brown's desk. Here you go Mrs. Brown he interrupted handing her the finished exam paper on black history month. Thank you Corey keeps up the good work and you'll be outa here in no time she replied. Um already outa here today. He thought quickly aight, I'll try Mrs. Brown. He turned to walk away and she said Cory then he turned around. Try to keep your nose clean ya hear she pleaded seriously. Yes ma'am I can do that, he assured then left outta class...

Chapter 6

"I WANNA BE WITH YOU"

BALAHMEAN HAD GIVEN MIA AND HER BEST FRIEND T-BIRD A RIDE to the fair. He gave her a hundred and thirty dollars to eat and enjoy herself with while having fun. She told him that T-Bird mother would be arriving to pick them up that night and that she would call and check in with him no later than eight o'clock. He kissed her on the forehead and said the usual goodbyes. Then he drove toward Tiffany house by Washington High School near west lake train station. Twenty minutes went by like clockwork and he was pulling into her apartment complex next to a black Lincoln Navigator where Tiffany lived with her only sister. He guessed they'd heard him before time cause Twon was standing in the doorway arms wrapped around her music and bass shook the ground uncontrollably as he cut off the car engine and got out wearing white Prada sneakers. An all-white robin outfit with an a-hat turned to the back of his head sideways. He wore two block gold earrings and a gold g-shook watch.

Bout time! She stated at him smiling childishly. Yeah right be for real girl. He stated heading up their driveway. They lived in a modest three bedroom apartment trimmed with steel blue and oyster shutters accented by an ornate wreath that hung from a brass hook on the front door. There was a chair on the porch next to multiple flower pots and sitting chairs. Roll up Twon laughed already high on another planet. You already know that he responded. Following him inside their well decorated house. The smell of chicken and macaroni and cheese. Balahmean took in the lovely smell of the well cooked food as they headed for the living room. Passing a large fish tank that sat on top of a black marble bookshelf. It was nice. He thought to himself taking in the exquisite architecture of their furniture. What took you so long anyway? Tiffany questioned as if she was his mother and chastising him. My mom's been dead most of my life. Who you think you are girl? Balahmean spit defensive. Fall back small back, my partna ain't no peon shawty, said Twon. Taking his partna side. Naw you fall back small back! Said a thick dark skin girl coming from the back room. Balahmean turned his head and almost felt certain that he was seeing things. You ain't got nothing to do with this shawty, this is an A and B conversation so C your way out my biz' ness lil buddie said Twon causing Balahmean to start laughing. What you laughing at? The girl asked placing her hand on her hip. Balahmean looked and saw that she was talking to him and stated. Listen baby girl um just a nigga trying to get in where I fit in. I don't want any smoke shawty? Thought so she added quickly blushing. It had turned out that she was the same girl he'd seen at the mall in Sak's fifth shopping store. Balahmean, this is my sister Tisha. And Tisha this is Twon best friend Balahmean. He from College Park. Tiffany introduced loving their chemistry... Balahmean had later discovered that Tisha was the bold and through bred bitch he was looking for. She was a bonafied hustler and knew the in's and out of the drug trade. Shoveling food into his mouth as fast as he could swallow it. Slow down boy! That food is not going anywhere any time soon said Tisha. Watching Balahmean stuff his face as

Twon did the same. You too boo. Tiffany told him unpleasantly. Pointing her finger.

I'm a big dog, not a tuna fish baby girl. Balahmean replied with his mouth full. Fuckin right I'm a mutha fuckin beast. Twon added watching them as they sat food untouched. Boy whatever you a starving bum what it looks like. Tisha corrected. Balahmean had five thousand in cash money in all hundreds and he pulled the bank roll of money from his pocket and sat it on top of the table. Next to the onion rings and stated money long like lil Wayne dreads never broke and smiled. Tisha and Tiffany just sat there silent watching them continue to eat. Finally Tisha began to eat and said kush got y'all with the munchies referring to the marijuana they'd all smoked before eating anything. Twon took long deep swallow of the koolaid from his cup and replied. Gots to know that. Tiffany finished her catfish, coleslaw and fries. Now she was ready for a piece of chocolate cake. I ain't even gonna lie boo. I'll love for you to be my ole lady, str'8 up! Balahmean spoke truthfully causing Tisha to smile. What you waiting for? Tiffany questioned sternly wanting them together more than anything. What! He replied confused. I said what are you waiting on boy? She's single Balahmean looked at Tisha quietly and said. She already my girl that a commitment he responded...

The next day Balahmean had taken Tisha advice and purchased five pounds of kush marijuana from their cousin Scott. He was from East Point. Scott had just come home a few months back from Georgia State Prison. He had served ten years to the door for armed robbery. Balahmean left the apartment to meet with Tisha. She'd told him about her ex-boyfriend having pounds of marijuana out in Mississippi. He left forty dollars on Mia nightstand and made his way out the house. Balahmean had given Tisha a hundred and fifty dollars to rent a car for several days. Pulling into their driveway he spotted a white tinted window Cadillac. Parking the car along-side the driveway. He climbed out dressed in all black from head to toe. He had a black duffle bag slung over his shoulder as he made his way up the steps and was about to knock on the door, when Tisha opened it wearing a pink bath robe. Pulled closed revealing parts of her lingerie. Hi, she greeted formally as he reached for an early morning hug. What's up sweetness, you up already boo? He asked kissing her on top of her forehead making her feel young all over again. I couldn't sleep she lied. Why not? He asked truly concerned. Cause you wasn't here to hold me, and keep me warm. She pulled free the ropes on her robe showing a sexy purple set of lingerie. He walked closer to her scooping her body into his arms. Gently as they mouth's met for the first time. She pulled off his little cap tossing it to the right side of the room. He carried her to the sofa and laid her down flat on her back. Kissing her neck on down to her breasts. He bit on her left nipple softly through the thin fabric of her lingerie.

Oooh! She moaned wanting to feel his every touch. He went from her nipples down to her stomach, before finally landing on her wet juicy pussy. He pulled off her lingerie leaving her legs hanging in midair as he stated. Still got some for me to eat ma? She nodded her head yes as he ate away at her sweet juicy pussy lips. Awww, God! The words escaped from her mouth. He blew softly onto her love button. And her hips arched upward to meet his face as he did his thang. She swore all kinds of things something she never did before. He turned her over onto all four in the doggy style position and entered her slowly. Her walls seemed to tighten in around his dick as he found her g-spot. Shitt! Your dick big she exclaimed almost out of breath. And your pussy super tight he replied. He speeded up his rhythm beating her wall in as she creamed all over his dick. I want you to have my baby, he submitted feeling himself build. Huh, um not ready she admitted half truthfully. He pounded away harder and ask her again even rougher than before. Until she submitted yes, yes I'll have your baby. Oooh shit! Don't stop she moaned busting another nutt for the second time. He groaned as he shot his load of sperm inside her hot, wet pussy. She grabbed a pillow and squeezed for dear life until finally she felt relief as his dick went soft. Oooh shit boy you got energy for days. She was cut off as they both felt piercing eye's glued on their backs and found Tiffany staring at them puzzled...

Chapter 7

"BLOODY SUNDAY"

THE MOON SHINED BRIGHT AS THE NIGHT WAS STILL AND SILENT. Only the sound of crickets and owls could be heard in a distance. Balahmean took a drag from the cigarette as he and Twon sat quietly eye's watching the big brick house. You ready bra? Always replied Twon sliding in the 30 round magazines into the bottom of his carbin 15.Let's do it said Balahmean clambering a round in his hand chopper that held a 20 clip. There was another clip concealed upside down that allowed him to reverse it if need. They both pulled down their skimask's as they exited the car and crossed over the rough tall land of grass. Disappearing into the darkness. They listened for any sound of voices or movements as they crept along the house. The time on Balahmean watch read 2:37 am. They jumped a ditch, and then ducked low through a bean field next to the house. If anyone was watching their eyes would be on the front driveway. They snuck in from the rear of the house. All lights were off. The house was still and quiet, not a creature was stirring. Through the shadows of the oak trees Twon crept over the wet damp grass until he came upon a side window. Bingo! He whispered to Balahmean pointing up at the window. Balahmean smiled devilish seeing that they had a way inside the house. He proud that they'd made it this far without any sound. Twon took a deep breath, then crouched low allowing Balahmean to climb up onto his back and grab hold of the half cracked window.

Balahmean pulled himself up into the window as Twon stood up full length. He climbed in and fell to his hands and knees. Balahmean listened as the dude flushed the toilet. He knew the man was Mario from the pictures she'd showed him that evening. Balahmean heard the sink being ranned and he gently slid back the shower curtains to find the dude in a pair of speedoes. That was tucked between his ass cheeks. This nigga crazy, Balahmean thought pressing the barrel of the chopper at the back of the dude's skull. Holla and I'll blow your shit all over this fucking mirror. He stated coldly seeing the shock and horror on his face. The dude replied by nodding his head by the way had a sewed on wig on it. Just get the weed, and you'll live to suck another dick, Balahmean assured. Alright just don't hurt me. I'll do anything he replied sexily tryna seduce him. Crack! Balahmean brought the barrel of the chopper down across his forehead leaving a thick gash as blood run down his face. "Aghh! Please!" He begged. Fuck nigga don't play, um solid my nigga. Do it again and you'll die, Balahmean aggressively replied. Matter fact put some mu'fucka bass in your voice when you talking to me any mu'fuckin way. Just don't hurt me; I'll get the weed for you. It's no pressure; he stated not wanting to suffer the consequences of dying for playing stupid. Go! No funny movements or game over. He assured following behind him with a handful of his gripped wig in his left hand as he held the chopper with the other. Twon had crept through the entire left side of the house when he'd heard footsteps come from a back room. The house was only a 3 bedroom home and he'd check two of them so far and came up empty handed. Still no sign of Balahmean creeping along wall he kept his carbin 15 held out in front of him scanning from left to right. As he made it halfway down the hallway the door to the left opened, and he instantly took cover behind a tall dresser that held a bird cage on top. A muscle dude came from inside the room but ass booty naked. Fuck! Twon mumbled heatedly.

Micheal! Micheal! The dude hollered receiving nothing but silence right here. He called out in response. Twon saw a dude come from in the bathroom wearing speedoes with Balahmean close on his heels. You know what it is homie, Balahmean spoke up seriously as the naked dude took off running down the hall. Twon stuck out his foot causing the dude to try a jump over it. The dude jumped his naked body into the air causing Twon to swing the gun and bashed him in the face knocking him completely out the air. Awww! The dude hollered falling to the floor with a thud. Get your bitch ass up! Twon then yelled pointing his gun at the dude's face. Blood raced down his face the exact same way it did the other dude. Pleaseee! Don't hurt him, Micheal pleaded sincerely as tears involuntarily came down his cheeks along with his thick red blood.

I'm gonna give you to the count of three to go locate them pounds, or you both dead. Balahmean said impatiently. It's out back! Micheal submitted. Aight lets go said Balahmean sternly.

Balahmean returned from the back yard carrying a large trash bag. He had a bag in both hands with a wicked grin. Where ole dude at? Twon asked not noticing him anywhere in sight. Out back he answered. Let's go bra we got the weed. It was confirmed by Balahmean. Thirty-seven thousand said Twon happily. Boom! Boom! Boom! Boom! Bullets from the carbin ripped through the dude flesh like paper spraying blood all over the thick brown carpet. Dawn! Balahmean mustered from the way Twon filled him with hollow tips.

Come on bra lets go, Balahmean stated tossing him the trash bag. They walked out the back door seeing the mountains country side with nothing but miles of nature around. Check this out Balahmean told him walking to the toolshed. Twon was once in shocked. Balahmean flicked on the light and Twon saw a puddle on of bloody clothes. He said. What the fuck! He stated feeling his heart beat rapidly. The dude wearing the speedoes was hanging from the ceiling by his penis. There was a hook from a metal chain hanging from his dick and balls. Man you sick bra. Um gone fool Twon stated. Hold up bra, did you see it? See what? Look, Balahmean pointed to a broken shovel stuck inside the man ass. Hell you got it going on shawty, fuck made you do him like that? Tisha told me he tried to rape her with a broom, so I returned the family favor. "Ya dig! "Say no more lets dip for them cop's come shawty. Aight, kool let me take some pictures first, he stated pulling out his iPhone snapping several pictures.

They then rushed away from the railed house as Twon squeezed lighter fluid through the grass making a trail all the way from the tool shed to the house. He took out A Newport and lit the cigarette and tossed it on the fluid. Wooooosh! The trail blazed instantly running a line of fire from the house to the shed. You hell shawty Balahmean stated climbing into the passenger seat as Twon brought the engine to life, then speed off leaving a bloody mess. Balahmean lit a Newport and cracked his side window for air. Man you losing your damn mind. Who the hell you trying to imitate? Mad max Twon questioned seriously.

Naw, um tryna be the black Jesus. Who else? Come on bra don't try me like that no more shawty, I feel offended my nigga, he replied snidely. Twon didn't even respond. He just stared at his friend in disbelief before crossing the line from Mississippi to Georgia.

They drove the entire way home silent neither saying a word lost in their own thought. Part of Balahmean did feel like he was losing his sanity. But the money kept him alive and focus. Pull over right here, let me buy some cigars. As they got off the expressway and turned in a Texaco gas station. Balahmean jumped out and ran inside the store and purchased a box of cigarillos and two Dutch masters and came back out. I love you like a brother and if you want out, then cool said Balahmean calmly...

Chapter 8

"UNEXPECTED"

It's been two days since Balahmean and Twon robbed Mario for 20 pounds of kush marijuana and 20 pounds of high price drop. They split str'8 down the middle on the weed. Balahmean allowed Twon to keep 19 thousand of the 37 thousand and he kept the other 18 thousand. Balahmean divided his share with Tisha the day before after introducing her to his sister. To his unsuspected surprise they got along very well. Take it Tisha told the salesman. She was a thin white older woman in her mid fifties. She was very nice and respectful. Okay ma'am, how soon are you trying to move in? She asked Tisha politely. Like yesterday she replied anxious. No problem here's your keys and my card with my home phone, cell and fax number. If anything needs to be fixed or repaired allow me to help and assist you in any way possible. We have the best maintenance and landscaping available at low prices she assisted. Okay ma'am no problem Ms. Barber replied Tisha. They watched as she climbed her frail body into her

BMW 745 and drove away. Yes she shouted with a gorgeous smile on her face "I love it, Mia agreed. Me too said Balahmean happy that they were happy. He had called her unsuspectedly and asked her and Mia to join him at site seeing a new house. I want one of them things too girl Tisha told Mia. One of what girl? She replied clueless one of them BMW. What you call it? She stated thinking of the name of the car. 745, Balahmean said admiring the beautiful 4bedroom 2bath home. Located in Lilburn, Georgia. In a fluent neighborhood. There was a pool in the back yard that went from 3 feet to 8 feet.

I'm gonna have the furniture store ship over the furniture first thing in the morning. Balahmean told them as they headed out to the new house. We'll just use the house on Victoria Street in College Park. As the trap and weight house. Tisha stated climbing into the car beside her man. Aight kool set up shop then baby cause everybody already know you sale weed. Just let them know we got nicks, dimes, two for the five, seven ounces and quarter pounds. I'ma has burglar bars installed on all door and windows from front to back. He said reversing the Chevy chevell out the driveway of the house. Say bra Mia called out from the back. What's up lil sis? Can we stop and get something to eat? Yeah where you wanna eat at. I'm hungry too. I got the munchies he replied laughing driving through traffic. Umm I want something from subway, she responded. Having an appetite for a philly cheese steak that's a bet. What you wanna eat baby? Same thing my sister-in -law wants eats slapping hands with Mia.

Two days later after finally moving all the furniture into their new plush home for the cost of ten thousand dollars. Today was Balahmean birthday and he was turning eighteen on August 9th. He was dressed in a Versace silk button down sleeve collar shirt, and farrogamo beach shorts and forragamo loafers. Tisha, Mia, Twon, Tiffany and him drove out to Canyon Ranch in Miami. "Swooosh!" Water splashed as Balahmean curved the jetski into a horrible uturn. He and Twon had been racing for over 45 minutes. The beach was jammed packed and overly crowded with women of all sorts. Some wore bikinis and some wore one-piece swimming suit. There where kids running along the beach throwing water balloons and flying kites in the wind. Balahmean zoomed past a couple making love in the sand. He smiled at them ignoring their love session as he flew by them with lighting speed. You better catch up nigga! He called back over his shoulder to Twon. Your lame ass cheated shouted Twon as he was gaining speed on Balahmean. As they near the beach where Tisha, Mia and Tiffany where all riding four wheelers across the sand. Balahmean looked back at Twon seeing he was slowly catching up to him. Oh hell no! Balahmean reviving back the throttle on the jet-ski gaining full speed.

Damn! Balahmean heard Twon yell as he closed in on the beach first. Your duck ass had to cheat me you lame as hell for that shawty. Balahmean playfully joked as they shared a laugh. Stop crying he said seeing Tisha sitting on the four wheeler. Mia and Tiffany were at the cheeseburger and hot wing stand ordering them something to eat. You see that? Twon asked pointing to a nigga with long thick dreadlocks. Who stood near Tisha running what looked to be game. She showed him off with a wave of her hand indicating that she wasn't interested in him. You need to fall back pimp said Balahmean. As they were about to get in an argument. Who you? The dude questioned with authority as if he had no clue. That's my bitch nigga! Now kick rocks for shit get real ugly partna. Straight the fuck up? Balahmean said with aggression in his voice, fuck this bitch nigga. He was cut short from the haymaker. Balahmean sent pounding against his jawbone hearing it crack. The dude stumbled backwards and fell over Twon Prada flip flops. Balahmean immediately began to kick him repeatedly in his stomach. Stop! Stop! Tisha managed to get him off of the dude before the coastguard and security arrived.

Sweat pouring down his face as he climbed on the back of the four wheeler while Tisha began to drive away. What just happened? Mia questioned already figuring her brother has done just what she had thought. She knew he was over protective about women. Bra just beat the shit out of ole dude for disrespecting his girl, said Twon. Snatching a hot wing from outta Tiffany's plate. In one quick motion...

Back at the Za Za Hotel the girls agreed to all stay while they went out. Balahmean wore all yellow linen suits with yellow mustard color gators on his feet. A yellow G-shock was round his wrist that held V.B.S diamonds around the rim. His hair was freshly cut in a lil Boosie fade. Twon wore money green Versace linen outfit, with green doo-doo spike Louis Vuitton sneakers. Bye boo Tisha called out kissing him on the lips. Aight ma said Balahmean. Love you daddy, Tiffany stated joking as their mouth met. Bye babygirl said Twon. Heading out the hotel door, don't get y'all ass in no trouble. God knows Florida will fly a nigga without evidence as Balahmean gave his sister Mia a kiss on the cheek. Can't argue with that sister that's why I gotta run this money up so I can put her through college. She wants to be a lawyer. Now you see why I have to do what I do. Just be safe, aight. Y'all try and get some sleep too. As he exited outside of their hotel room.

Boy pleases! We bout to get fucked up! Tiffany spit out the door as they made it to the silver elevators and rode it down to the main floor. They crossed the lobby and headed to the valet desk where they asked for the car to be pulled around. As the valet guy pulled up in a 2010 black four door rover and hopped out dressed in a red velvet top vest and black clad pants. Here you are homie? Balahmean and Twon pitched the black man a ten dollar tip. Thanks you gentlemen. I appreciate it. Heading off to fetch another car for a white couple. Balahmean got behind the wheel and fired up a blunt of dro. We bout to ball all night Twon as the smell from the dro invaded his nostrils. Oh yeah! You can believe that as they agreed shoveling a stack of one dollar bills into the armrest. Balahmean pulled into the parking lot of a club called Diamond on the beach of Miami. He parked beside a donk on 26 inch rims. This bitch stupid, park right here. Twon spotted a woman in a black leather cat suit as she stood bow legged as if her clothes had been painted on her by Pablo Picasso the Spanish paint artist. She was super thick, that ass was phat Twon replied climbing out of the Land Rover. Balahmean and Twon made their way across the parking lot into the VIP line. Where they had to pay one hundred and fifty dollars in cash to enter. The other line was crowded with all types of women short, tall, thick and skinny. They stood waiting to be let inside the club the rapper Jay Smooth fo 'real and T-Money was in the building with all kinds of bad bitches.

A white Lamborghini pulled in and stopped with two unknown trucks right behind it. Mr. Bigg Time the rapper and his crew emerged from the expensive cars. Ice shining like crushed pieces of glass. Balahmean and Twon stood amongst the crowed VIP toasting too the good life. Also commemorating the hard times of the past and putting them to rest. As they popped bottles living it up among themselves. Jay Smooth came over the mic and said what's up? What's up? I wanna give a big shout out to someone special today Happy B-day Balahmean! G.T.O. In the mu'fuckin building. Balahmean come to the stage home boy. We bout to pop bottles like never before nigga! Jay Smooth shouted throughout the club.

The crowd went crazy as he continued to shout Balahmean name. He stood there shocked not knowing what to do until Twon smiled and said I wanna say happy B-day nigga. Holding up a bottle of Rozay. Twon lead the way to the stage and introduce him to the entire G.T.O.. He dipped Jay Smooth, fo'Real and T-Money then handed him the microphone A.T.L and G.T.O in the building. Gangsta's taking over in this bitch forever! Free my nigga "POPEYE "! G.M.C. Get money crew in this bitch making it rain. Get rich or die broke! Balahmean yelled into the mic as women flashed their breasts and tossed lingerie onto the stage floor. Jay Smooth and Balahmean pulled up to a table as Future new smash hit "Honest " came over the club speakers and Twon reached in his inside pockets and pulled out the three thousand dollars in one dollar bills and began flying them out into the crowd. G.T.O and G.M.C. Bitch! He yelled out over the music. And I'm just being honest. He shouted as he saw the crowd going crazy about the money raining. Balahmean couldn't deny it this was the best birthday party ever. I'm never going to be broke again. He thought as he let go a fist full of money. The bills looked like a bunch of fireworks on July 4th as they flew through the air like crazy.

Balahmean thought he'd saw a flash of silver from inside the crowd, but thought against it. He threw the remaining bills into the air as Future next hit came over the speaker "I Rock Gucci, I Rock Bally, At The Same Damn Time!" On the phone cooking dope, At the same damn time! Selling white, selling loud, at the same damn time! Fucking two bad bitches at the same damn time!"

Boom! Boom! Boom! Boom! Gun shots ranged out loudly throughout the club deafen the music. Balahmean saw a member of G.T.O. Fall to the stage in a heap of blood and at that instant. Boom! Another shot was fired and this time it sent Balahmean twisting backwards, agh shitt! He mumbled in pain as he felt his shoulder burning. Damn he hollered out as Twon pulled him back stage amongst the guests. He aight fam? T-Money asked taking a liking to Balahmean in less than one night. Look like he took one to the arm he was silenced as Balahmean brought his arm up holding his favorite 38 special. Boom! Boom! Boom! His bullets slammed into a dark skinned nigga with dreads who Twon found to be the dude from Miami Beach. The nigga was sent flying across the floor as security bum rushed the crowd. Let me take that while you get him to the car. I'll meet you outside homie T-Money spoke grabbing Balahmean gun T-Money had ditched his crew and rode shot gun while Balahmean rested on the back seat, the entire drive to Miami Memorial Hospital near Poken Bean Projects. Twon called Tiffany and relayed the message to meet at the hospital immediately.

After a couple minutes of waiting a black man in his early thirties approaching them calmly dressed in surgical scrubs. A mark hung from his neck. Are y'all relatives of Cory Taylor? Asked the doctor who name tag read Doctor Brown.

Yes said Mia and Tisha responded at the exact same time. Okay good news he's alright. Only flesh wound but he's lost quite amount of blood is the news bad. So far he will be just fine thou said the doctor. When can we see him? Twon standing next to T-Money who was very quiet most of the time. I was afraid you'd say that since it's only a flesh wound I'll allow you all to see him. I was told he'll be released in the next few hours. But what the heck, he smiled leading them down the hall to room number 716.

Thank you doc said Twon heading into the room first. Your welcome sir he replied walking off giving them privacy.

They walked in to find Balahmean pulling off his hospital gown, dressing in his regular clothes which had speckles of blood on them. He heard some noise and stunned around nervous thinking he'd been caught red handed by the doctor. Leaving anytime soon Twon joked seeing his partna in good health and condition. His right shoulder had been stitched closed and was wrapped and bandaged. Mia and Tisha both rushed into his arms. I'm not leaving you again said Tisha. Tears in her eyes, me too said Mia. I know you was a trouble man just couldn't make it through one night, not even on your birthday. Good to have you back homie, T-money chimed in bitterly. Balahmean recognized him for the very first time and couldn't understand why he was there helping him. No doubt homie, I appreciate the love fam Balahmean spit dapping him up with a hand shake. What's understood ain't got to be explained my nigga, said T-money assuring.

True shit he replied likens T-money in a brotherly way. He could tell that he was younger than him that caused Balahmean to wanna fuck with young dude. I'm gonna start calling you problem child said Tiffany laughing. Nawl, call me the Black Jesus he joked back. Everyone busted out laughing at his remarks. I'm ready to go. This is T-money. My girl Tisha and my lil sister Mia. Oh also my girl sister Tiffany. He introduced them. What's up y'all? I know who you are T-Money we used to go to the same elementary school together. Don't you rap with G.M.C., get money crew Mia announced? Yeah, I knew you looked kinda like someone I know I just could not put the face with the name. He responded lustily....

Chapter 9

"WHAT THE FUCK!!"

A WEEK AND HALF HAD GONE BY SO QUICKLY, AND THE TRAP HOUSE Balahmean and Tisha had on Victoria Street was doing numbers. After placing burglary bars on the doors and windows everything seemed to just fall in place. There were a few remaining competition and his enemy Black had suddenly become one of them. Mia birthday had just passed a few days behind her brother's and she was now sixteen years old. T-money and Mia had become acquainted in the past few days. It started with him buying her a diamond ring that had his name imbedded in the center of the expensive jewelry. T-money was sixteen years old and was soon to be seventeen in a less than a few months. Balahmean did not approve of Mia having a boyfriend but since he had love for the young fella. He recommended that they were grown and was capable of doing what they wanted to do. With or without his recommendation. Black had become a little more thoughtful at lowering his prices and not only was he gaining clientele. He was also slowly stealing Balahmean as well. That alone had given Balahmean and Tisha the acknowledgment of seeing him as an official threat. The entire scenario had him a bit uncomfortable for various reasons, and he was certain that Black would soon become a problem. T-money and Tisha were both at the trap house as Balahmean sat quietly at his plush black hard wood computer desk. His arms had been positioned in a shoulder sling, and it was time that he got back to business. Aight bra holds it down. I'm bout to run to the store real quick and get a few extra weed bags and something to eat. Tisha shouted to T-money who was at the living room sofa playing the PlayStation 4. Do you need me to ride shotgun big sis? You know I got that hammer? He replied nawl I'm good lil bra I got the hammer too she started laughing. Kool, say no more be safe cause nigga out there lurking on a slip up you feel me. T-money was always concern about Tisha well-being and protection. True true I feel you lil nigga. I been doing this shit for years but I'll take that into consideration fo'sho! Now you be safe. She stated heading for the door. Tisha climbed in the black Land Rover and speed away from the house. She was listening to Rihanna new hit single "Pour it up, pour it up. That's how we ball out! Throw it up! Throw it up, watch it all come down!"

She drove bobbing her head to the music as she took a long drag on the Dutch master blunt filled with dro. The city was busy and the sun shined bright as people headed about their day. A black S.S Impala could be seen a few cars back behind her. If only she'd been paying attention to her surroundings. She drove through the stop light and made a right turn on Main Street in College Park and drove past Captain D"s. As she was pulling into the gas station the black impala swerved up beside her on the diver side. Two masked men jumped out running full speed toward her truck. She looked and almost panicked as T-money words attacked her mind like a lion. Get out the car bitch! The first masked gunman yelled yanking open her diver side door. She screamed and hollered grabbing onto the steering wheel for better support. Only a few people entered and exited the gas station so she raised hell to be left alone. Get off me! She shouted loudly kicking the gun man in his chest causing him to stumble backwards and almost fall flat on his back. "Agh, Bitch!" He yelled aggressive as the other dude came running around the other side of the car in attempt to help his partner. Oh my god she thought before quickly locking the passenger door. "Bitch open this door before I kill you hoe!" The dude was furious at seeing he'd been beat to the punch. Spit flew from his mouth. She gathered her bearing and grabbed hold of her Prada purse reached inside bringing out her baby glock 40 that held 12 shots. Pointing the gun at the gunman who was trying to grab hold of her. She saw him look up. Boom! The first bullet struck him in the eye splattering blood all over the inside of her driver side door. The dude fell into a heap of blood. Dead on impact. Fuck! She heard the other gunman yell as he rushed back to the impala snatching open the passenger door. Tisha jumped out firing. Boom! Boom! Boom! Bullets crashed into the windows shattering glass all over the gas station parking lot. Sceeeeere! The impala burned rubber speeding outta the gas station. People rushed to her in attempt to assist seeing the entire scene take place before there eye's. Are you okay ma'am? An older man asked. Is you hurt, said another woman who looked to be her age. She just stood there quiet staring at the dead gunman. A crowd of people gathered around the dude's body. Some scared, feared and even cried she tucked her license glock into her Prada purse and pulled out her cell phone. She dialed Balahmean cell and got him on the first ring. She gave him a run down on what had just taken place and he told her not to go anywhere cause that would place her freedom in jeopardy. He asked was there any cameras and she replied yes. She told him that there were many witnesses who'd saw the whole thing go down, and willing to testify on her behalf. He replied by telling her to stay put and not to say anything until he'd paid a lawyer. He would have a phone call placed to the lawyer legend Dennis Bolton to represent her at whatever the cost was. She ended the call with Balahmean saying I love you. Tisha stood amongst the crowd nervous as she fought her best to hold her composure and gather her bearings. Her heart speed rapidly as her adrenaline kicked in full gear. An older woman stood by her side holding her hand

and whispered. Everything gonna be alright child. Just have faith and be thankful to still be alive. God knows it could have been much worse than it was. The woman was in her mid fifties. She was slightly on the chubby side and bearded wrinkles amongst her skin. She put you in the mind of Oprah. Thank you she replied softly still kinda shocked from the attack. Ten minutes passed and a white and red ambulance from Grady memorial hospital arrived. A swarm of police cars invaded the gas station just as Balahmean red chevell speed in behind them. He immediately parked the car and attended to her needs. You okay baby? Are you hurt ma? He stated dramatically placing his arms around her as the detective headed their way...

Tisha was taken into custody and transported back to College Park prescient and mirandized. Dennis Bolton had arrived within minutes holding a briefcase. Dressed in a black tuxedo made by Marc Stanley. Witness had followed the squad of police cars back to the prescient to testify and like the older woman said she was the first one to testify on her behalf. Luckily there was an off duty police officer who'd been at the gas station when everything took place, or she would be spending over night in College Park jailhouse on the south side of Atlanta. She was able to be released after all investigations were done. She filed a statement and a self-defense report. Dennis Bolton had argued his client had no past history or record and there for was not a flight risk to the state of Georgia.

Unfortunately he was pushed to call judge Knowels, Fulton County courthouse representative and gain Tisha a signature bond with an account of being charged with self-defense murder. She was given an assigned court date hearing as they placed a leg monitor around her ankle. You are free to go Ms. Williams said Sgt. Smith the supervisor for the day shift. Thank you she replied with a smile as she grabbed her purse. Good thing your weapon was registered or you'll be doing time for the gun alone, said Dennis Bolton as they headed outta College Park city jail holding center.

I know right, thank God she quickly responded as they walked out the front door where Balahmean was sitting smoking a cigarette on top of his car hood. He looks frustrated and appeared to be on another planet than the one's they were on. He heard footsteps growing closer and she turned to see them heading his way. Jumping off the hood of the car he rushed for her embraced. Tiffany, Mia, Twon and T-money were all back at his new house in Lilburn, Ga.

You good ma? He asked kissing her on the lips passionately for what seemed like hours. Dennis Bolton coughed letting them know that he was still present. As an on duty officer passed by them in acknowledgment. Oh! Damn! Balahmean pulling out ten thousand in cash handing it to the lawyer. He had told Balahmean he'd take the case due to the tragedy. And that it would be a good case cause he could beat it with no problem. Not to mention it would be good on his agenda and case record. Thank you for everything. We really appreciate the help and assistance said Balahmean sincerely knowing that it could have been ugly. Sure no problem. Just make sure you are on time next week for the hearing is all we need to prove she's not a flight risk he stated genuinely. Oh no doubt we'll be there. My words are all I have and to me it's all I need, Balahmean replied shaking his hand as they departed ways.

Tisha had told them in her statement that the gunmens were trying to rob and kidnap her. For what reason? She didn't know......

Chapter 10

"DONE DEAL"

TWO DAYS HAD PASSED AND TISHA COURT HEARING WAS COMING the following week. The twenty thousand Balahmean had given the lawyer. Put his cash at a lower level even though they still had a few pounds to cover half the dough, twenty thousand was a lot of money. He'd given the lawyer ten up front and ten after Tisha released from custody. Twon and Tiffany had taken a flight to Ohio to visit her aunt who'd lost her sister to HIV. Tisha was saddened because she was not able to leave the state. But Balahmean helped keep her spirits at an all-time high. Mia had been accepted at Spellman College in the west end of Atlanta. Because of her excellent grade point average. She was the only one and the youngest girl to score the highest test results in the entire school. Balahmean and T-money had been on a lurking spree to locate the people behind Tisha accident. It had been rumored that the nigga Tisha killed was supposed to be the cousin of his enemy Black. Tisha had also confirmed that the gunman had been driving the same kinda SS impala his father drove.

T-money made sure to keep two or more cars back as they followed Meat. Meat was Black older brother and partna in crime. He had just come from making his last round from all three trap-spots. Being they had five in all. Two in East Point, one in East Atlanta and two in College Park. Meat was driving a tan Camaro get rental with tinted windows. He pulled into the wings supreme restaurant drive through and stopped to order at the menu. To give his order. Pull up right here Lil bra Balahmean spit pointing to a white pick-up truck that sat parked in front of the restaurant. Aight he replied parking the car next to the truck. T-money held an A.R 15 in his lap as Balahmean opened the passenger side door gripping his 30 shot glock 40 in the palm of his hand. He closed the door back and crept low across the night parking lot. The restaurant was pretty much filled except for the outdoor lot where little people emerged carrying their food.

A red bone saw Balahmean creeping across the lot and passes their car. Oh my God! The woman said recognizing him from the neighborhood. Balahmean looked up and spotted her staring at him. He immediately made a sign with his index finger for her to keep quiet, as he whispered, I got you! To her holding up his hand gesturing money sign she nodded her head, which was done in micro braids. Her face was that of a teenager. Even though she was in her twenties. Balahmean moved around the building toward the drive-in window where meat sat at the window waiting for his food. Balahmean rushed up alongside the car and in one motion snatched the driver door open. Pull off or I will split your shit. Wide open! He stated calmly not wanting to draw attention. "Aight man!" "Aight!" He yelled back defenseless fear flashed all over his face feeling his heart increased. "Move over nigga!" He said with a wave of the gun. Here's your food sir, oh my God! Help! Screamed the woman seeing what was taking place. Shut up bitch! Balahmean drawing another gun from his waistline. Might as well rob her too. He thought. Balahmean slid the slide window open with force aiming the gun at her face. Run that check bitch, before I wet your ass up!

She hit a few buttons and the register popped open and she emptied it from all contents and handed him the fist full of bills. Good looking out, he replied. Boom! Boom! The woman stumbled as the entire restaurant began running ducking and screaming for help. She fell backwards into the metal grill knocking her head against the counter.

The glock 40 was still aimed on Meat as all commotions went down. He jumped out the car and took off running. Boom! Boom! Boom! He released multiple shots hitting nearby cars as one of the bullet slashed into his left leg. Balahmean reached inside the Camaro and grabbed the gym bag from the back seat. T-money sat patient as he heard the gunshots rang out. He saw Meat limp from around the corner of the restaurant and stop at a Malibu. There was a red bone and another brown skin girl sat waiting on their friend to come out.

Got your bitch ass! T-money mumbled thinking the mission went badly. He climbed out the car leaving the door halfway opened as he crouched low to the ground.

Call the ambulance please! T-money heard him pleading holding his leg as blood pored over his shoes.

Help on the way homie! T-money lied causing Meat to spin around. Blatt! Blatt! Blatt! The A.R 15 tore chunks of flesh from his body knocking him up against the Malibu.

Awwwww! Evvvvvve! The red bone and her friend screamed in horror as Balahmean came dashing around the building. Holding the gym bag over his good shoulder. I was gonna let your bitch ass live, said Balahmean. Sending a shock wave throughout the parking lot as the glock 40 bullet pierced Meat face. "Rest in peace." Scooter spit harshly. Balahmean looked at T-money for a split second and they both smiled a devilish grin before turning their guns on the screaming girls in the car. Bullets ripped through the windows blasting glass all over their faces as they couldn't do nothing but suffer the unsuspected tragedy....

They heard a woman scream follows by the ringing alarm of the restaurant.

Balahmean turned as T-money headed to the car and saw a girl hold-ing a bag of hot wings that she unwillingly dropped to the ground seeing. How they'd just disintegrated her friends. "Wrong place wrong time!" He yelled to the girl seeing fear in her eyes. He brought the barrel of the glock into view as the girl stood there in total complete shock. Click! The gun was empty. Saved by God baby girl, he spoked as T-money swerved the car alongside him. He climbed into the car and to his surprise T-money turned the car around and stuck his gun out the window. "Sorry!" He stated. Boom! She dropped on impact...

The streets of Atlanta, College Park, and East Point were on fire as the news flashed different locations of murders, robberies and home inva-sions. Balahmean was now almost five hundred thousand to the good and T-money saw his first hundred racks. They'd hit four of Black trap house's killing everything that required life of breath. Tisha knew he and T-money was the cause of the chaos. But she refused to say anything not because she didn't care or was scared. It was that she knew what had triggered him to go hard the way he did. The money, cars, clothes and jewelry made him this way. Guns and hoes even the life style itself pushed him to go harder that he did.

Your honor, I now ask that my client may walk away uncharged as the tragedy at hand already. Has scared her permanently. Her gun was there by legal of registration. She had the right to carry a weapon, so to the fact that the area she live in is known for its bold robbery. Just look at how they tried to high jack, rob and kidnap this beautiful woman. The incident took place in self-defense over ten witness has testified on my clients behalf and still the district attorney is pushing for any type of conviction said Dennis Bolton making his point known "I object your Honor!" District attorney Paul Coward yelled decline Mr. Bolton representation.

Bamm! The judge banged his wooden gravel. I will call for a ten min-utes break, then I'll be ready with my final decision said Judge Knowles. As he exited the courtroom. Don't worry Mrs. Williams you're gonna be a free woman with no felony none what so ever on your record. He assured her.

She nodded her head in approval as she glanced back at her mother Tracy, Mia, Tiffany, Balahmean, Twon and T-money. They all were present for her support. It had been two months since the tragedy happened and she was ready to get this last session over with completely. She looked back again this time catching her eye contact with her lover. He was dressed in a white Italian tuxedo with red button down under shirt and red velvet Italian loafers on his feet. She thought he was ever so sexier with a suit than clothes. "All Rise!" Said the bailiff as judge Knowles entered from his chamber. The court room was packed to the capacity. To where people had to stand up at the back of the court the entire session.

I here by the court of Fulton county state of Georgia, move this case to be dismissed and the defendant take rehabilitation class to rehabilitate! He stated banging his gravel. The whole entire courtroom erupted in cheers and applause as Tisha jumped to her feet excitedly as Balahmean scooped her off the floor. Yes! She shouted as she saw the look on the D.A. Face. You did it baby. She yelled loudly as her mother, Tiffany, Mia, Twon and T-money all rushed to her side. Naw ma, we did it baby girl. He corrected spinning her around in circles. Happy that they'd won the case on time...

Chapter 11

"CLUELESS MIND"

AFTER TWO WEEKS OF REHABILITATION CLASSES. TISHA THREW A party at their house in Lilburn, Ga. she invited some trusted friends but mostly family. She wore a house of Deleon outfit made by the singer Beyoncé with Prada heels. Her hair was in micro twists and pulled up into a bun. She also had on some earring made by Alexander Mc-Queen. She was gorgeous and everyone kept complementing her of favoring the dancer Tip Drill. Food was prepared and scattered all over two long tables with white sheets covering them. There was chicken wings, French fries, onion rings which where her favorite. Fish, burgers, hot dogs, ribs, pizza and different types of chips, cookies and cakes.

There was a little over twenty something people there. Balahmean had cameras installed all around the house. One was mounted directly over the front porch and another on both sides of the house. Balahmean also put one camera in the backyard. He had a safe vault built into their bedroom closet floor that you'd never know was there. Unless you were to strip the whole floor of carpet. Hey baby Balahmean softly in her ear wrapping his arms around her waist from behind. Hey! She spoke turning for a kiss on the lips. Having a good time? Of course Daddy my family here and my best friends and not to mention my knight in shiny armor. She laughed. Oh really I hear that he joked. Y'all can do all the baby making later after we're gone said her mother Tracy. Hey mama! Are you enjoying yourself? She asked glancing around seeing everyone talking and having a good time. Of course, I got my son-in-law here to make sure of it. Isn't that right baby she asked him pinching his jaws playfully? She like Balahmean, yes Mama Tracy you know it. He answered agreeing.

Oh lord, boy! What have I told you? Call me Tracy nothing more, nothing less she snapped joking. How's everybody? Mia announced walking hand in hand with T-money. Looking like Future and Ciara. Everyone responded with their own remarks and replies. They all talked and kicked it before Tisha grabbed a wine glass and a spoon and banging it softly.

Excuse, excuse me everyone can I have everyone attention please! She asked respectfully as everyone got quiet. I wanna say thank you all for coming, and for supporting me through my trials and tribulations. It's nice knowing that I have friends and family that I can count on in time of need. I wanna say thank you for all love and comfort, most of all I wanna thank my man. So with that being said. I want you to know that I'm two months and 3 days pregnant. Balahmean was sipping rozay from a glass and almost choked when she mentioned being pregnant. Everyone turned to look at him and he smiled assuring knowing it's what they wanted...

After the party Tisha thrown everyone was exhausted as they all began to leave and depart ways. Balahmean was genuinely emotional by the toast Tisha made last night. Her being pregnant wasn't really shock to him cause they'd been wanting to make a baby. But how she delivered the news is what caught him off guard. He felt naked and vulnerable. But his obsession is what drives him to conceal his insecurities and perfection. He wanted to make sure that his baby grew up in a better environment than he did.

From fifty-one storage in the air the city lights were amazing. Balahmean stood out on the expensive hotel balcony staring over the entire city. He had come up on the very streets hustled its blocks, chased its bold scandalous women's. He was Atlanta south side officially, from jumping over the gates at the local train stations, to shooting dice in the roughest projects there was. Dressed in clad and Versace slacks, and a matching vest. He fit in nicely as he walked into their penthouse suite. The penthouse suite held a Jacuzzi in the nearby floor. Tisha was getting dressed in her house of Deleon outfit as he walked in. You okay? Mia spit. Yeah, just had a lot on my mind and had to clear my thoughts baby. I hear that Daddy so does that mean you're gonna get out the game? She questioned with a serious facial expression that demanded an answer right away. I don't know Ma. I'm not sure. I still have unfinished business, but I can promise that after this last and final shit. I gotta handle, we gonna be straight forever. That way I can fall back with no worries about expensive. He submitted truthfully grabbing her by the waist and pulling her closer toward him for a passionate long kiss. They broke their kiss and Tisha grabbed her purse and said, you promise me? He looked at her intensely in the eyes for a split moment then respond. I promise baby girl.

His word was sincere and that's all she needed to hear. Better she joked playfully gathering her things and checking their cell phone for missed calls and messages.

Yeah right, you know what's up babygirl? He stated calmly picking up his car keys from the nightstand. How bout we eat out for breakfast? Aight where to he replied clueless. She thought for a second or two and said I-hop. Kool let's go baby, he said heading for the door with her close on his heels. They came out the penthouse suite into a small hallway before the elevator with multiple numbers on its door frame. They stepped on rode down to the main floor kissing and touching ready for round three. Exiting the elevators she headed toward the checkout desk to return there penthouse keys. Thank you ma'am said a skinny young black woman in her late teens. No problem, Tisha replied handing her a ten dollar tip as they turned around and headed out through the revolving doors of the downtown hotel in Atlanta...

Knock! Knock! Knock! T-money tapped on the door. He was dressed in all black with a black fitted cap pulled low over his eye's. In his right hand held a Russian Uzi with a 32 round magazine hanging from the bottom. Who dat! A male voice called from the other side of the door. Knight! He called back hearing the dead bolts being unlocked as the door swing open. Knight who? T-money aimed the uzi cutting him off in his sentence.

Knight mare! You holla and I'll push your shit back all over the floor nigga, T-money said coldly. Gun at face level.

Take it easy fam, the dude replied as Balahmean and Twon rushed in at that exact moment. Y'all fool know what it is! Said Balahmean already scanning the room with the Barrel of his M-16 assault rifle. How many y'all in here? Twon questioned already knowing there were four of them inside the house.

Three... three of us he lied.

Whap! Whap! T-money unsuspected bashed him over the head with the barrel of the uzi. Drawing blood instantly. Ahhh! Hold up fam he cried in pain holding his head while Balahmean and Twon rounded the corner of the dining room hall. Fuck you lying for? You must be trying to pull a death stunt nigga. We already know how many y'all in here stupid ass nigga. T-money keeping his machine gun fixed on his head. Go that way, Balahmean whispered to Twon hearing voices come from the nearby room. Twon nodded his head acknowledging his words.

Peeping around the corner. Balahmean saw three niggaz all sitting at a table which had large amounts of cocaine on it spreader out into different piles and sandwiches bags. He searched around the room in search of the last dude and felt a cold piece of steel press against his skull.

Balahmean body stiffened from been caught slipping and he silently began to spray. Long time know see huh, Black spit nice of you to stop by. I been looking for you, you killed my brother he stated. Not knowing he was buying time for someone to save Balahmean life. I finally got your bitch ass. Boom! Boom! Bullets crashed into the wall causing him to look back and that gave Balahmean the opportunity he'd prayed for. He quickly rotated around knocking Black into the wall as he bent to grab his m-16 from the floor.

Pow! Pow! Pow! Black bullets missed him by an inch and a half as he took flight into the next room.

TaTat! TaTat! TaTat! Balahmean dropped a heavy set dude on impact as he rounded the corner never knowing what hit him.

Bok! Bok! Bok! Pussy said T-money unleashed multiple shots into the dude chest and neck. As he slammed up against the wall. Boom! Boom! Boom! Boom! One of the other nigga's fired at Balahmean making him duck behind the flower vase and T.V set. Shit! He exclaimed ready to bounce back from around the corner wall.

Boom! Boom! Boom! Boom! A hell fire of shots sent the dude who'd just been shooting at Balahmean across the carpet floor. TaTat! Tat! Balahmean bullets silenced him forever. He died with his eye's wide open. He getting away bra, Twon stated firmly. Pointing toward the open back door. Damn! Y'all get the work, weed and money. I got him! Balahmean shouted rushing out behind Black. Who'd obviously been hit cause of the trail of leaking blood? He followed the trail out the door, he ran around the back and saw the Black SS Impala on 24 inch Crome Davins Rims and almost tripped. Almost tripped over a rock. Damn it. He mumbled in search for Black who was losing quite amount of blood. Balahmean looked and saw Black leaning up against the car garage holding his stomach. Where blood oozed between his fingers. I guess you got me huh? Black spit gun aimed at the floor. Drop the pistol homie, said Balahmean. Demand deadly pointing his M-16 at his forehead. Dancing the infrared beam across Black face. Who car is this? Balahmean desperately wanted to know. Black looked over at the Impala and smiled. You don't have a clue? Do you? He asked with a puzzled expression look on his face. From an unhealthy fixation, stop playing games nigga! You oughta be trying to swerve your way up out this shit! He replied tried of the mystery and games.

Take a wild guess then, Black replied pointing his gun up into the bottom of his chin. Poww! Pieces of brain and skull fragments went splattering across the garage side wall as Black body went limp and slid down leaving behind a trail where he last stood. Fuck! Balahmean yelled bending down and reaching into his lifeless body pants pocket. Pulling out a stack of money. He removed the pinky ring from Black pinky finger and walked off toward the house starring at the impala.

His father had the same exact car, color and rims and that did nothing but intensified his curiosity. He stopped in mid stride and inspected the left side bumper where his father car had a permanent dent in the front. As he bent and admired the car, he saw exactly what he was looking for. He froze for a moment letting the shock register his mind as Twon and T-money came up behind him holding large bags. Come on fam, what's up T-money asked feeling there was something wrong from the way Balahmean was quiet. What's up homie, said Twon curiosity scanning him from head to toe. He did it bra, that pussy nigga did that shit! Balahmean spit in anger knowing Black had killed his father and now killed himself. There was nothing he could do about it. That coward killed my dad bra, he replied pointing at Black dead body...

It had been six months since they raided Black main and last trap house in College Park. They recovered over three hundred thousand worth of heroin and cocaine, and over two hundred and sixty five grands in cash money. They split the money three ways. The product was done the same, down the middle. They all had their own ways of getting money.

Twon had nearly four trap house. T-money invested his money on a home based studio for his rap career, and Balahmean owned a pool hall and a barber shop in East Point. Peanut had turned him on to his plug, known as connect in most cities and states. The plug was Columbian and he was a very wealthy man. He'd told Balahmean he'd give him fifty bricks of pure Columbian cocaine if he ranned his product throughout the United States.

He replied taking the once in a life time offer, and was now the face of Atlanta. He started fucking with Big Grip and yellow bio from the organization G.M.C.

His clientele expanded from Atlanta to New Orleans, New York, Detroit, Chicago, Texas, Tennessee and Mississippi. Tisha owned and managed her beauty salon on Old National. Mia got accepted in Spellman College, but later enrolled in Clark Atlanta. Tiffany bought a day care center in College Park off Main Street. Balahmean came out the plush and well established mansion that Ruben his Columbian plug owned. The mansion was 51.000square feet. The home was built with dirty money. It was the mansion of families who had been rich for generations. Visit anytime you want, you're entitled to what's ever mind is yours son, said Ruben stretching out his hand wide enough to indicate his way of living.

He had multiple armed guards standing and scattered all over the outside and inside his home. Naked women moved along as if there was nothing to see. Thanks for the offer, but I'll reconsider for now. It was a delicate pleasure of you to invite me and my girl, Balahmean replied nodding in Tisha direction. Who was now waiting on him to say his good byes? She leaned patiently against the limo alright son travel safely said Ruben as they shook hands. Appreciate Balahmean called back headed towards pregnant Tisha who's stomach was poking out like a broken bone.

Come on Daddy before we miss our scheduled flight. Anxious to get back to Atlanta she was astonished. We not taken an airplane back Ma, you can relax

Babygirl. Balahmean replied rubbing her stomach with his hands as they disappeared inside the stretch hummer limo. They popped a bottle of Rozay to their lifestyle.

Does this mean you're out of the game now Daddy? She questioned thinking their trip was for him to end all ties. Yes babygirl, he lied as they both got comfortable so gone by and they were pulling alongside a beautiful and fabulous Lear jet the same color the ocean at night. Wow! It's beautiful; she exclaimed climbing outta the limo. Heading towards the jet steps.

I know right tell me bout it, he joked as they headed up the stairs and was greeted by Frank Jr the copilot. He was dressed in black suit pants, dress shoes and a white collar shirt with a red neck tie.

They settled into their seats amazed at the expensive jet. There was full stock bar of liquor, sodas and bottle waters. A small refrigerator was mounted above a cabinet next to a white mini microwave. The leather seats were in grave with Louis Vuitton stitching as well as the carpet on the floor of the jet. The interior was plush and deck out. Prepare for takeoff. Please buckle your seat as well. We'll be lifting off in exactly two in a half minute, Frank Jr. stated assumingly as he walked off.

At exactly 2:30 p.m. They were indeed flying over Columbia. It's beautiful down there; she said pointing outta the Lear jet. Small window at the ocean below. It was indeed lavish. How many times you gonna say that baby. I know he joked laughing as she playfully punched him in his left arm. Shut up don't be funny babygirl. I'm being sarcastic and realistic. I have told you a million and one times the way here, he joked. And you need to shut up! He playfully joked as they shared a laugh together. The jet landed at a private script in College Park. They were carrying their belongings when outta nowhere a massive squad of police and F.B.I cars speeded upon the Lear with their lights flashing as well as the sirens. What the fuck! He shouted feeling everything crumble. Baby what's going on? She demanded. Seeing all the F.B.I suits. This supposed to be the last drop. Don't nobody know bout this but me, Peanut and Ruben. He yelled in frustration.

Last drop! You said you were done after dis last meeting? Tisha replied calmly feeling used and betrayed. Tears began to fall as she stared him in the eyes. That fool ain't right Babygirl! Balahmean started to scream and spit... Who? Who? Ain't right she begged as the sirens blazed? F.B.I.! F.B.I.! Screamed an agent flashing her gold badge at them. She withdrew her small glock special edition hand pistol. He threw his hands up into the air as if he was surrendering. Then quickly shoved Tisha as far away as he could. Drawing his twin glock's he began to fire. Boom! Boom! Boom! Boom! The F.B.I sent a hail of bullets into his body but not before he dropped the first agent who'd flashed his badge. Noooo! She screamed dropping to her knees. He ain't right baby girl, he ain't right! Was his last final words.

SNEAK PREVIEW

BALAHMEAN LIVES BY THE CODE.... PART TWO

Awwww, shit! Balahmean moaned as Tisha head bobbed up and down on his dick. She played with the tip of his head with a silver tongue ring. Her head was like a jumping pogo-stick. Going up and down. He stood up and flipped her around and positioned himself behind her from the back. His dick stood hard and erect as he slid it up and down her pussy. Then entered her with ease. Ooooooohh baby! Give it to me!

She moaned through gritted teeth as he pounded her roughly gripping a handful of hair. Which was nicely done. They body's slammed together with a back to back smack. She screamed and moaned loud as he continued to beat her pussy into submission.

I'm coming, she screamed gushing cum down side of his manhood, me too baby girl. He groaned shooting a pool of sperm inside her pussy.

He kept up his rhythm and speed up until his dick went limp. I see you had a lot built up since my last visit. She told him putting on her clothes and straightening her hair.

Hell yell, I been waiting since forever, he joked. Balahmean was sentenced to life. His lawyer Dennis Bolton had been telling him that he gonna win an appeal, and possibly get him out free. Balahmean was in housed at Atlanta Federal Penitentiary near Thomasville "project of Atlanta ". He was allowed conjugal visits do to the fact that he and Tisha was now married by law. Tisha had delivered a baby boy whom she'd name Joseph Jr. He was now three and a half years old and looked just like his father...

The Saga 2 be continued for part 2 "Balahmean lives by the code"